WARTHOGS PAINT

A MESSY COLOR BOOK

BY **Pamela Duncan Edwards**

ILLUSTRATED BY
Henry Cole

Hyperion Books for Children
New York

For Judy Edwards—the artist in the family!
—P.D.E.

To Dot Pat, the world's best
third grade teacher.
—H.C.

Text copyright © 2001 by Pamela Duncan Edwards
Illustrations copyright © 2001 by Henry Cole

Printed in Hong Kong

This book is set in 18-point Bookman.
The artwork for each picture was prepared using pen,
colored pencils, and watercolor paint.
First Edition
1 3 5 7 9 10 8 6 4 2

Library of Congress Cataloging-in-Publication Data
Edwards, Pamela Duncan.
Warthogs paint : a messy color book / Pamela Duncan Edwards; illustrated by Henry Cole.—1st ed.
p. cm.
Summary: As some warthogs spend a rainy day painting their kitchen, they make a mess and learn about mixing colors.
ISBN 0-7868-0470-X (trade)—ISBN 0-7868-2412-3 (lib.)
[1. Warthog—Fiction. 2. Color—Fiction. 3. Painting—Fiction. 4. Stories in rhyme.]
I. Cole, Henry, 1955– ill. II. Title.
PZ8.3.E283 Wat 2001
[E]—dc21
00-036944

Visit www.hyperionchildrensbooks.com

The warthogs can't go out—it's such a rainy day—
But everyone's tired of warthog play.

"There must be something to do," they cry,

As they watch the rain falling from the sky.

"I've got an idea! Why don't we start

To paint our wall with warthog art?

"All colors can be made, I've heard it said,
As long as we have some yellow, **blue**, and **red**."

"Good idea!" they cheer, and everyone rushes
To find the paint and fetch the brushes.

Splish! Bend low. **Splash!** Stretch tall.

"Let's paint **red** on our kitchen wall."

Run up the ladder, up to the top.

"Be careful there! Don't let the pot drop!"

The ladder is wobbling! "Danger! Look out!"

See the big yellow puddle and the little yellow snout.

Splish! Bend low. **Splash!** Stretch tall.

"Let's paint **yellow** on our kitchen wall."

"Here I come. Please let me through.

It's my turn now to paint with **blue**."

Crash! "Whoops! Whee! This is funny.

I'm mopping up the floor with a bright **blue** tummy!"

Splish! Bend low. **Splash!** Stretch tall.

"Let's paint **blue** on our kitchen wall."

"Excuse me, please. I don't want to slip.

All stand back! The paint's going to tip!"

"What a terrible mess! But see, it's clear:

Mixing **blue** and **yellow** makes **green** appear."

Splish! Bend low. **Splash!** Stretch tall.

"Let's paint **green** on our kitchen wall."

"**Orange** is my favorite. Can I make that?
Hey, watch out! I've tripped on the mat!"

Splosh, splat! "You are a clever fellow.

You've made **orange** by mixing **red** and **yellow**."

Splish! Bend low. **Splash!** Stretch tall.

"Let's paint **orange** on our kitchen wall."

This eager painter isn't looking where she's going—
Across the floor **red** and **blue** are flowing.

"Watch red and blue as they mix and muddle.

Soon we'll be paddling in a **purple** puddle."

Splish! Bend low. **Splash!** Stretch tall.

"Let's paint **purple** on our kitchen wall."

They've had a good time on this dull, wet day;
Warthog painting has chased the gloom away.

They've worked so hard and they've had such fun—
See their big warthog **rainbow** and their little Teddy sun!

We're primary colors.

We can help you make all the other colors.

Get ready to mix!

When you mix two primary colors you make a new color!

Green! Orange! Purple!

Which two colors were used to make the ladder green?
Which colors were used to color all the other things?

Which warthog is holding a primary-color umbrella?

Which warthog has an umbrella made from red and blue?

What's your favorite color? Is it a primary color? If not, try to find out how to make it!